ZAC ZOLTAN'S
MAD MONSTER
AGENCY

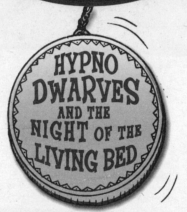

HYPNO
DWARVES
AND THE
NIGHT OF THE
LIVING BED

Knife and Packer

ORK

Meet Josh Flunk – a regular school kid.

And his best friend, Spencer Topps.

They live in the town of Everyday, which is an everyday kind of place. Except . . . unlike most towns Everyday has a DARK side. From time to time phantoms creep and spectres loom. But these aren't your common, everyday monsters, these are MAD monsters and they are REAL!

Getting rid of them requires much more than an 'everyday' solution. Time to find out about the Mad Monster Agency.

When Josh Flunk's great-great-great-grandfather, Franklin Flunk, bought an ancient Egyptian sarcophagus from a junk shop, he didn't realise it was going to change his life, and his family's life, for ever . . .

When Franklin took it home and dusted it down, he noticed that an object had been left at the back.

He stepped inside to discover a bizarre walking stick with an ivory skull-shaped handle that had fiery rubies for eyes . . .

And that's when the lid slammed shut behind him. There was an eerie moaning, a strange glow and then a loud BANG!

When Franklin stepped out he had transformed into ZEBADIAH ZOLTAN – MAD MONSTER AGENT extraordinaire!

From that day on, every time the eyes on the walking stick started to glow it meant there was a Mad Monster crisis.

The Mad Monster Agency passed down the generations, until Josh's father was mauled by a zombie mouse and developed a phobia for all things monster. The next in line was, you guessed it . . .

Franklin Flunk would hurry to the secret room he had built beneath his house, step into the sarcophagus, and become Zebadiah Zoltan once more – ready to protect the town of Everyday.

HOORAH!

Josh Flunk, aka Zac Zoltan, the latest (and youngest ever) head of the Mad Monster Agency!

ZAP!

Along with his partner, Spencer Topps, alias the gadget king, Dr Brains . . .

And trusty assistant and Troll, Odd Dan the Odd . . .

Zac Zoltan fearlessly fights Mad Monsters of all sizes (and shapes).

Although there are lots of imitators . . .

AUNTY EDITH'S NASTY MONSTER SORTING-OUT ORGANISATION

there is only one MAD MONSTER AGENCY.

In fact a Mad Monster might just be stirring at this very moment . . .

Chapter One of . . .

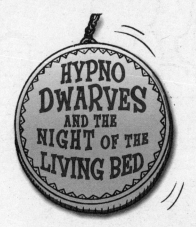

1

It was a big day in the history of Everyday. From now on there would be no more waiting for buses, no more traffic jams, because Everyday was getting the world's first ever high-speed Gyrotrain!

'So what is a "Gyrotrain"?' Josh Flunk asked his best friend and all-round brainiac Spencer Topps. It was the last few days of the school holiday and Josh and Spencer had joined the crowd at the Grand Opening.

'It's like an underground train system, only quicker,' said Spencer. 'Although it uses groundbreaking transport technology, the science is actually very simple: it operates through a combination of intense air pressure and powerful magnetic fields.'

As usual when Spencer said something was 'very simple', it wasn't . . .

'Although I'm surprised they went ahead with building it,' he continued. 'The soil is surprisingly porous here, meaning it is prone to collapse.'

But before Josh could quiz Spencer about the geological risks to Everyday's Gyrotrain system, the crowd went quiet and all the VIPs leapt to their feet as a large, shiny black limousine glided into view.

'Who's in that car?' asked Josh.

'It must be the reclusive owner of Onyx Enterprises,' said Spencer. 'That's the company who built the tunnels and the Gyrotrains. I assume he's here for the opening ceremony.'

'But he's not even getting out of his car,' said Josh.

SNIP!

A small, bent hand with podgy fingers emerged from the window. The Mayor placed a pair of scissors in the hand and with a single SNIP! the ribbon was cut.

'Many thanks to Maximillion Onyx,' said the Mayor, addressing the crowd. 'The Everyday Gyrotrain is now officially declared OPEN!'

The crowd cheered and began to pour through the gate, everyone eager to get on one of the first trains, but Josh and Spencer held back.

'Look – he's already driving away,' said Spencer. 'I suppose running a multi-billion-pound industry means there's always work to be done.'

'Mmm,' mused Josh who was less impressed. 'I've got a weird feeling about this place . . .'

VROOOOM!

They entered the station and joined the long queue of people snaking through the ticket hall. It certainly looked impressive. Huge marble columns supported the ceiling and the walls were carved stone. But as Josh looked around at the cold, forbidding hall, he suddenly noticed a strange, small wooden door, out of keeping with the grand scale.

'I wonder where this leads?' said Josh, 'And who could fit through it? It's minuscule.'

'It must be the entry to the service tunnels,' said Spencer. 'The Gyrotrain system needs access tunnels for water, electrics and ventilation.'

'I think we should take a closer look,' said Josh. 'My Mad Monster Agent senses are tingling.'

'This wasn't made in any factory,' said Spencer. 'The door handle looks like solid gold and this design looks like some sort of big cat and an eyeball set in a jewel. But why would you put something like this in a ticket hall?'

'It's all weirdly elaborate,' said Josh, squinting.

But as he examined the tiny door more closely, Josh felt a tap on his shoulder. He turned around to discover a large, familiar and very nasty-looking face.

'Hey losers, come to enjoy the new Gyrotrain?' scoffed Boyston Fitch, the school bully. 'Of course, my dad was chief engineer on the project so I've already had a private tour!'

'It's very impressive,' said Spencer.

'Yes, we've got the plans at home and there are all kinds of special rooms and tunnels,' continued Boyston. 'Hey, why don't you have a look down this one!'

2

Boyston was about to open the miniature door and shove
Josh and Spencer through it when the whole station was
plunged into darkness!

'EVACUATE! EVACUATE!' boomed the public address
system. 'THIS IS AN EMERGENCY!'

'We need to get out,' said Josh. 'The exit door. Now!'

Although daylight was clearly visible through the exit,
that didn't stop Boyston taking centre stage.

'Everybody follow me!' he shouted. 'I know this place
like the back of my hand!'

People poured forward as Boyston bossed people
about.

'Everyone stay calm! There are some stairs that way,
then turn left and head out!'

Making their way reluctantly to the exit, Josh and Spencer were suddenly stopped in their tracks by a dreadful, high-pitched squeal. In the darkness they could just see Boyston's lumpy outline – and he was on all fours!

'Hey, Boyston's got his leg stuck,' said Josh. 'Dangerous stuff this, being a hero!'

'Help!' cried Boyston who had been bundled over in the stampede. 'My leg got caught in an air vent . . . It's awfully dark in here! Somebody please help!'

No matter how hard they pushed and pulled, Boyston would not budge.

'Looks like the emergency services will have to fish you out,' said Josh, finally admitting defeat.

As Josh and Spencer stepped outside, a team of firemen with rescue gear stormed past in the opposite direction.

'Apparently some clown got his leg stuck,' shouted one. 'Did you see him?'

'You can't miss him – he's the big, loud boy wailing at the top of his voice,' said Josh.

'Go easy with that axe!' chuckled Spencer.

3

With the Gyrotrain out of action, Josh and Spencer took the bus back to Josh's house instead.

'Everyday may not have a functioning Gyrotrain system yet, but seeing Boyston stuck in that air vent certainly made up for it,' said Spencer.

'Strange, though, that such an expensive project should go wrong on opening day,' said Josh. 'And that the alarm went off just as Boyston was about to open the mystery door.'

At home Josh's mum had plenty of questions too. She wanted to know all about the new train service.

'So is it all modern and shiny?' she asked. 'It's going to be so much quicker than walking.'

'I don't think that place will be opening any time soon,' said Josh. 'There was a power cut and everyone was evacuated!'

'And I was planning to go to my keep-fit class by Gyrotrain,' sighed Mrs Flunk. 'Oh well, maybe it will be fixed by next week.'

When they finally made it to Josh's bedroom, he and Spencer immediately saw that the eyes on the ivory walking stick were glowing red!

'I could tell something was up,' said Josh crawling under the bed as fast as he could.

'You know I don't really understand why your mother wants to travel by Gyrotrain to her keep-fit class,' said Spencer as he dodged the usual collection of dust balls, old toys and socks. 'The health and fitness benefits of brisk walking are often underestimated.'

'And so are the benefits of brisk crawling,' said Josh, as he made his way as quickly as possible to the hidden entrance.

When they reached the trapdoor that led to the Agency, Josh tapped out a secret code and it slid open. The two then jumped on to the chute that hurtled them down to the ancient Egyptian sarcophagus.

'Hold tight!' cried Josh.

'I am holding tight!' said Spencer.

The sarcophagus wobbled and throbbed as it worked its magic – there was a loud BANG and the pair leapt out into the Agency. Josh had transformed into Zac Zoltan, Mad Monster special agent! And Spencer was now Mad Monster gadget expert, Dr Brains!

But instead of finding Odd Dan the Troll, the third member of the team (who actually lived in the Agency), monitoring the computer screens or examining data, he was kneeling on top of the desk waving a feather duster!

'We saw the eyes glowing,' said Zac. 'We got here as soon as we could!'

'What are you doing *on* the desk?' asked Dr Brains. 'Shouldn't you be *behind* it?'

'Thank goodness you guys got here!' gasped Odd Dan. 'This place is overrun with Mad Monsters!'

'Where?' asked Zac as he scanned the room. 'I can't see anything!'

4

But as Zac and Dr Brains tried to locate the Mad
Monsters, even weirder things were occurring back at
the Gyrotrain station . . . involving the school's very own
hyperactive PE teacher, Mr Derrick.

Mr Derrick loved exercise. Running, jumping, press-ups – he couldn't get enough. In fact he had so much energy that he had set up a business to keep himself active in the evenings and weekends too: Derrick's Super-Speedy Deliveries. So when Mr Derrick landed a huge contract he was absolutely delighted. He arrived to make the first pickup, and his delight quickly turned to confusion.

'I've been to warehouses in some pretty strange places,' chuckled Mr Derrick as he bounced in, 'but in a Gyrotrain Station? That's a first! Hey isn't this the ticket hall? When is this place reopening?'

'We're not paying you three times your usual rate to ask stupid questions,' said the foreman, a very small, grumpy man with a very long beard. Mr Derrick noticed that like all his colleagues the man was wearing sunglasses – underground!

'Of course not,' said Mr Derrick, who decided that, unlike most of his clients, these pocket-sized men were not into light-hearted banter.

'My boss is insistent that the packages go out immediately,' said the foreman, holding up a small box.

'And you want me to deliver one of these to every single man, woman and child in Everyday?' said Mr Derrick as he looked up at the vast mountain of boxes.

'Yes, in the next 24 hours,' said the foreman. 'In fact I'm going to make your life a bit easier by delivering the first one for you.'

The foreman handed Mr Derrick a box.

'Go on, open it up.'

'An alarm clock?' said Mr Derrick, holding up the timepiece. He'd never seen anything so beautifully made – in fact he was in a daze just looking at it. 'It's, it's beautiful. I'll put it straight on my bedside table. But can I ask why you want every single person in Everyday to have one? Is it some sort of publicity stunt?'

'That's a good question,' said the foreman. 'There's a letter inside every box explaining the promotional details and that the mystery donor will reveal himself soon. But now here's a question for you: why haven't you started delivering? You've got 24 hours, remember. In fact I now make it 23 hours and 57 minutes!'

'But it will take me hours even to get all these on the back of my lorry,' said Mr Derrick, as he flexed and stretched his muscles.

'Don't you worry about that,' said the pint-sized foreman. 'We'll load them up.'

'But, but there's only three of you,' said Mr Derrick, looking around the room. 'And if you don't mind me saying so, er, you're not the biggest . . .'

The foreman clenched his teeth and made a low, growling sound – Mr Derrick got the message and star-jumped back to his cab.

But as he sat there, no matter how hard he squinted into his wing mirror, he never once glimpsed the vertically challenged team amongst the blur of boxes. All he knew was that somehow the three tiny men had loaded his lorry in the twinkling of an eyeball. But Mr Derrick had no time to ask any questions – he was bursting with energy to get delivering . . .

Derrick's Super-Spee Deliverie

The other thing Mr Derrick did not see was that one by one they had removed their sunglasses, to reveal not two, but one enormous eye! They then turned to stare at the boxes which rose gracefully to the air and floated into the back of the lorry!

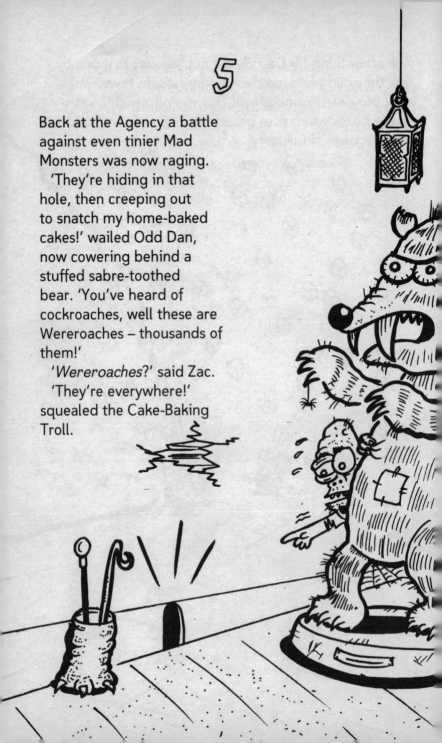

5

Back at the Agency a battle
against even tinier Mad
Monsters was now raging.

'They're hiding in that
hole, then creeping out
to snatch my home-baked
cakes!' wailed Odd Dan,
now cowering behind a
stuffed sabre-toothed
bear. 'You've heard of
cockroaches, well these are
Wereroaches – thousands of
them!'

'*Wereroaches*?' said Zac.

'They're everywhere!'
squealed the Cake-Baking
Troll.

Zac and Dr Brains could see hairy cockroaches with large fangs scurrying in and out of a mousehole.

'They certainly appear stronger than the average cockroach,' said Dr Brains, watching whole sacks of flour and huge jars of pickled fruit being transported towards the wall. 'Although a typical domestic cockroach can stay alive for up to two weeks without a head, and can survive a nuclear explosion.'

'This is no time for facts,' said Zac. 'We've got to stop them!'

'This should do it,' said Dr Brains, holding up a silver candlestick holder. 'Like their distant cousin the Werewolf, they should hate anything silver.'

Grabbing the shiny antique Zac dodged oncoming Wereroaches and jumped over a column of them scurrying towards Odd Dan's pastry pantry.

'It may not be a silver bullet but this should do the trick,' he cried, luring the Wereroaches back towards the mousehole using one of Odd Dan's triple-caramel muffins. The mini Mad Monsters took the bait, Zac threw the muffin into the mousehole, the roaches scuttled after it and he plugged the hole with the silver candlestick! 'I think we got all of them,' he said triumphantly.

'Not quite all of them,' said Dr Brains, holding up a jar, 'I'm going to keep hold of this one – for scientific purposes.'

'What?!? Get rid of that hideous creature at once!' insisted Odd Dan.

'The lid's tightly shut,' said Dr Brains, as reassuringly as he could. 'I'm working on a new gadget – the Mad Monster Trans-Species-Inter-Communicator – or MMTSIC for short . . . It's going to allow me to talk to Mad Monsters! This Wereroach will be the perfect guinea pig, if you know what I mean . . .'

With the last remaining Wereroach safely locked in Dr Brains's workshop, Odd Dan finally went to get the Wereroach Fact File.

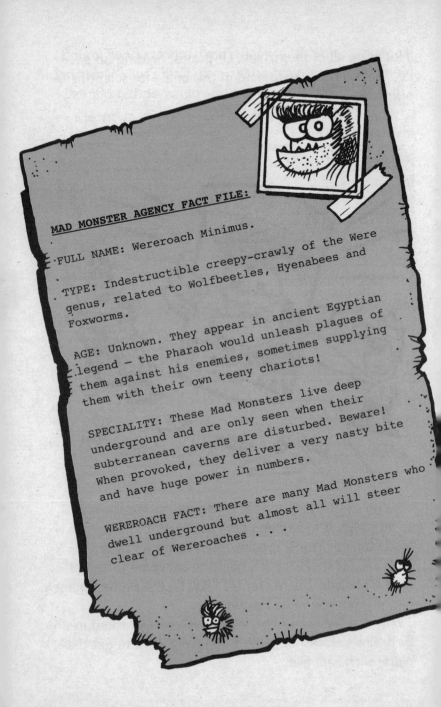

MAD MONSTER AGENCY FACT FILE:

FULL NAME: Wereroach Minimus.

TYPE: Indestructible creepy-crawly of the Were genus, related to Wolfbeetles, Hyenabees and Foxworms.

AGE: Unknown. They appear in ancient Egyptian legend — the Pharaoh would unleash plagues of them against his enemies, sometimes supplying them with their own teeny chariots!

SPECIALITY: These Mad Monsters live deep underground and are only seen when their subterranean caverns are disturbed. Beware! When provoked, they deliver a very nasty bite and have huge power in numbers.

WEREROACH FACT: There are many Mad Monsters who dwell underground but almost all will steer clear of Wereroaches . . .

'For some reason there have been lots of underground Mad Monsters around lately,' said Odd Dan. 'Yesterday I'm sure I saw a Foxworm in one of my potted plants!'

'That's interesting,' said Zac. 'Do you think it's got something to do with the tunnels they've been digging for the new Gyrotrain system?'

'Digging tunnels!?!' said Odd Dan. 'No one told *me*. If I'd known they were digging tunnels, I would have barricaded the Agency. There are far too many varieties of subterranean Mad Monster.'

'You need to keep more abreast of current affairs,' said Dr Brains. 'You're so out of touch down here. It was the Grand Opening today.'

'More like Grand Closing!' said Zac. 'There was a power cut and the place had to be shut . . . Curiously, it happened just as Boyston was about to open a suspicious-looking door.'

'It wasn't the kind of door you'd expect to find in a modern train system,' added Dr Brains. 'There was a very unusual design carved on to it.'

'We wondered what the design stood for,' asked Zac.

'Do a sketch of the carving and bring it to me later,' said Odd Dan. 'I've got some SERIOUS tidying up to do – my kitchen has been savaged!'

But Josh and Spencer soon forgot about the strange door and its carving. It was the last few days of the school holiday and they were having far too much fun to worry about Mad Monsters (although Spencer couldn't resist occasionally popping down to the Agency to work on his Mad Monster Trans-Species-Inter-Communicator with his new friend Scarab, the Wereroach).

6

When Josh's brand-new alarm clock rang, it was time to get up for the first day of the new term. Normally he'd feel a little bit excited, but today he just felt strangely tired . . .

'Breakfast is ready,' said Josh's dad, who looked like he hadn't slept too well.

'I need more coffee,' said his mum blearily.

Josh met Spencer at the street corner and noticed that he was yawning his head off too.

'My new alarm clock kept buzzing and buzzing,' said Spencer. 'But it took me ages to get out of bed.'

'So you got a new alarm clock too?' asked Josh. 'It seems that everyone in town got one - Mr Derrick must be making a fortune!'

As they walked through the school gates, they saw a large crowd had gathered in the playground – at the centre was Boyston Fitch.

'If it hadn't been for me, hundreds of people would have been trapped underground,' bragged Boyston. 'The world needs heroes like Boyston Fitch!'

'So how do you explain your bandaged foot?' chuckled Josh. 'Maybe everyone would like an eyewitness account?'

Boyston, glared at Josh and Spencer threateningly. Fortunately, the school bell rang for assembly.

The whole school seemed to have slept badly: even the Headmistress kept yawning. But when it was time for Show and Tell everyone perked up – especially when they saw what Spencer had brought in.

'Behold Scarab, the obedient cockroach!' said Spencer proudly. His Trans-Species-Inter-Communicator had been working well and the Wereroach was now trained to obey his every command (in exchange for mini chocolate-chip biscuits).

'Look, he can walk along this perilous tightrope, jump through this hoop and even do a backflip!'

The other kids were stunned and amazed – only Boyston noticed that the cockroach had an unusually hairy face.

'That's not some sort of Mad Monster, is it?' boomed Boyston. 'Because if it is then me and my friends will have to EXTERMINATE it!'

Boyston and his gang considered themselves to be Mad Monster hunters, but all they ever succeeded in doing was getting in the Mad Monster Agency's way.

'Er, no,' said Josh, who was always nervous that, despite being stupid, one day Boyston might work out who they really were. 'Scarab does, er, have an unusually hairy face, er, that's because he's, er . . . wearing a false beard – it's part of the act . . .'

'Yes, he's got five assorted beards, all in different colours,' said Spencer. 'And a clown suit . . .'

Luckily at that point the Headmistress said it was time for everyone to go to their classes – and Josh and Spencer's secret identities remained a secret (for now).

'That's the last time I bring a Mad Monster to school,' said Spencer, as they entered the school gym for their first class of the day – PE. 'It's just that Scarab gets so bored being in the Agency on his own all day – Odd Dan won't go near him.'

'Strange,' said Josh, noticing what their teacher was doing. 'It looks like Mr Derrick's having a nap . . .'

7

Over the next few days everyone seemed to be getting more and more tired. But the final straw came when Josh and Spencer got home from school one day to find Josh's parents fast asleep at the breakfast table still in their pyjamas. They hadn't moved all day!

'Wake up, wake up!' shouted Josh. His parents finally roused themselves.

'Who's for more cereal? Toast anyone?' said Mr Flunk.

'Er, Dad, it's 5.15 in the afternoon . . . you must have been asleep all day,' said Josh.

'Really? Well I'm still tired, I'm off to bed,' said Mr Flunk.

'See you in the morning,' yawned Mrs Flunk.

'This is definitely not normal,' said Spencer. 'I've been feeling more and more sleepy ever since we went to the opening of the Gyrotrain.'

'That reminds me,' said Josh. 'We never did show Odd Dan that sketch of the carving. I'll just have a quick nap, then we'll pop down to see him.'

'I think we should go now,' said Spencer, even though he quite liked the idea of a sleep himself. They crawled slowly under the bed to the secret trapdoor . . .

'Great to see you, guys!' boomed Odd Dan, who didn't seem to be tired at all. 'I'm getting some unusually high readings on the Mad Monsterometer.'

'More Wereroaches?' asked Dr Brains. 'Hyenabees?'

'Stronger than that,' said Odd Dan, as he fiddled with the dials on the Mad Monsterometer.

'I think it's time we investigated this,' said Zac, handing Odd Dan the sketch of the cat-and-jewel logo.

Odd Dan scrutinised the picture.

'I've seen that somewhere before,' he said fiddling with one of the warts on his cheek. 'I'll need some raspberry trifle.'

Although Odd Dan had a vast knowledge of Mad Monsters, he always needed some of his own home cooking to really get his brain going.

'Flying trout, possessed banjos,' muttered Odd Dan as he scoffed his trifle messily. 'Ah yes – the Lion's Eye!'

'The Lion's Eye?' said Zac. 'What's that?'

'It's an extraordinary gemstone, one with great powers,' said Odd Dan.

'Powers?' said Dr Brains. 'What powers?'

'I'm not sure exactly,' said Odd Dan, flicking through the Fact Files. 'It's not been seen for centuries.'

'So whoever built that door is in some way connected to the stone?' said Zac ominously. 'Onyx Enterprises?'

'But they're a legitimate business,' said Dr Brains. 'Why would they be involved with an ancient gem? They dig big tunnels and build Gyrotrains.'

'I'm no expert on Mad Monster jewels but I know someone who is,' said Odd Dan, holding up a Fact File. 'She might be able to help. Maybe you should pay her a visit?'

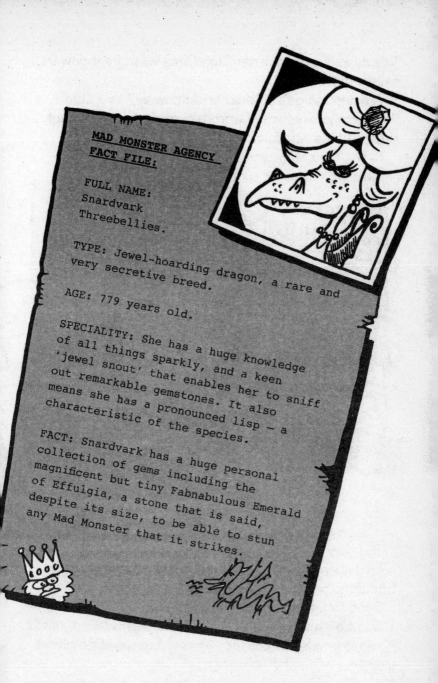

MAD MONSTER AGENCY
FACT FILE:

FULL NAME:
Snardvark
Threebellies.

TYPE: Jewel-hoarding dragon, a rare and very secretive breed.

AGE: 779 years old.

SPECIALITY: She has a huge knowledge of all things sparkly, and a keen 'jewel snout' that enables her to sniff out remarkable gemstones. It also means she has a pronounced lisp — a characteristic of the species.

FACT: Snardvark has a huge personal collection of gems including the magnificent but tiny Fabnabulous Emerald of Effulgia, a stone that is said, despite its size, to be able to stun any Mad Monster that it strikes.

'Great, we'll go tomorrow,' said Zac, stifling a yawn. 'I need a nap . . .'

'You need to go and see her right away,' said Odd Dan sternly. 'She's not far from here. She lives in a cave, hidden in the woods of Everyday Park.'

'To the Mad Monster Bikes!' said Dr Brains, as enthusiastically as he could.

'I'll call ahead and let her know you're coming,' said Odd Dan. 'Snardvark doesn't get many visitors.'

'Good thing you're wide awake, Odd Dan' said Zac.

'Don't be too long,' said Odd Dan. 'All this talk of Mad Monster jewels has got me nervous. I'm sure I heard the scurrying of another Wereroach.'

As Zac and Dr Brains cycled to Snardvark Threebellies'
cave, they couldn't help but notice how quiet Everyday
was.

'You'd expect to see people out jogging and cycling,'
said Dr Brains.

'Look a bit closer, Brains,' said Zac, as he pointed out
sleeping joggers slumped on park benches, cyclists
snoring over their handlebars and slumbering dog-
walkers being dragged along by their dogs . . .

In fact even the most energised man in Everyday was feeling the effects!

My morning fitness routine is a complete mess, Ethel. I've only managed 30 finger press-ups and I can barely jog my normal half-marathon. I never thought I'd utter these words but, but . . . I feel tired!

Zac and Dr Brains arrived at Snardvark's cave.

They knocked and knocked at the front door, but there was no reply.

'Maybe she's out for the evening?' said Dr Brains. 'This place gives me the creeps. Why don't we come back tomorrow?'

'We need to see her now,' said Zac. 'We've got to get to the bottom of this.'

Zac was surprised to find that he could gently push the door open. He called out for Snardvark, but there was no answer.

A light glimmered at the end of the corridor.

'This way,' said Zac. 'She must be in.'

'Are you sure about this?' quivered Dr Brains. 'I've never met a dragon before.'

'She's a friend of Odd Dan's,' said Zac as they slowly edged towards the light. 'That makes her a friend of ours.'

As Zac and Dr Brains entered the cave at the end of the corridor they were dazzled by walls encrusted with hundreds of lustrous gemstones. Slumped in front of a roaring fire was Snardvark – fast asleep!

'This place is amazing,' said Zac as he shielded his eyes from the sparkling stones.

'We've got to wake her up,' said Brains.

After first whispering and prodding gently, Zac eventually had to resort to shouting to wake the sleeping dragon.

'What? Where am I? Who are you?' she rumbled when she finally came to. 'Oh yeth you muthst be Zac and Dr Brains. Odd Dan told me you were coming. What can I do for you?'

'We wondered if you could tell us about the Lion's Eye,' said Zac. 'Odd Dan said you are the world's leading expert on Mad Monster gemstones.'

'Thath's very kind of him,' lisped Snardvark. 'I thee mysthelf as a thelf-taught amateur. Been collecting curthed rings, lucky brathlets and enchanted crowns for years. Now then . . . the Lion's Eye. Thit down and I'll tell you a thtory . . .'

The Story of the Lion's Eye

Many Mad Monthters have long coveted precious thtones. But one thtone has always been coveted above all others – the Lion's Eye. It has the most alluring power of all. You thee, whoever owns it can hold mankind under their thpell . . .

It is believed that it was once the thentre-piece of the crown of the legendary King Noymaxx III – who enthlaved the world with its power.

Then a group rose up againtht him . . . and theized the curthed gemthtone – the fearthome Thstone Dragons. They didn't want one of the earth's underground treasures used for evil purpothes. To enthure it would never fall into the wrong hands again they hid it, frightening off all those who tried to find it.

They guard it to thith day, deep, deep underground . . .
thomewhere thoo deep it can never be found!

For hundreds of years Mad Monthters tried to find it,
but the Thtone Dragons had done thuch a good job that
gradually, over the thenturies, the Lion's Eye became no
more than a firethide thtory told to thcare children . . .

So beware of
the evil King
Noymaxx!

But my 'gem thenses' tell me that the thearch has
rethumed in earnetht. Whothoever theeks the thtone
will only be doing tho for evil purpothes. They must on
no account be allowed to possess it – that would thpell
disathter for us all!

'So you think some sort of Mad Monsters are looking for the stone?' said Zac ominously. 'But how does that explain why we're all feeling so tired?'

'No idea, but then I'm too exhauthted to think for very long,' said Snardvark. 'In fact if you don't mind I need to go back to thleep – I was having a delightful dream about the opal mines of the Gratheknee Hills.'

'You've been a great help,' said Dr Brains.

'We must head back to the Agency and work out our next move,' added Zac. And with that they zoomed back to the Agency as fast as they could . . .

9

When Zac and Dr Brains arrived, they discovered that a full-blown Mad Monster Crisis was underway.

'There are reports coming in from all over town,' said Odd Dan, as he manned the giant panel of video screens. 'The Mad Monsterometer blew up!'

'What's going on?' asked Zac as he zoomed in on a screen.

'Everyone seems to be suffering from chronic sleep deprivation,' said Dr Brains, scrutinising the readings.

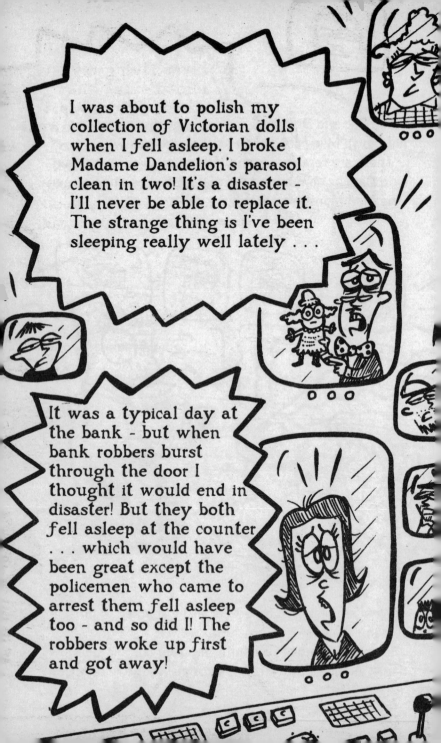

'They've all got similar stories,' said Odd Dan. 'If this carries on Everyday will grind to a complete halt!'

'Snardvark believes that some sort of Mad Monster may have begun searching for the Lion's Eye,' said Zac. 'It must be connected to all this sleepiness – but *how*?'

'And *how* does this tiredness affect everyone at once?' asked Dr Brains.

'Not quite everyone,' said Zac, trying not to yawn.

Odd Dan seemed to have more energy than ever and was managing to read incoming reports, dust the screens and eat some of his home-made double-decker chocolate eclairs, all at the same time.

'His sleep pattern isn't showing any adverse signs at all,' said Dr Brains.

'I think the first part of our mission is simple,' said Zac. 'Whatever it is that's making everyone tired . . . it isn't affecting the Agency. Get your sleeping bag, Brains. We're spending the night down here!'

10

As Zac and Dr Brains bedded down for the night, strange things were happening deep, deep beneath the snoring town . . .

The new Gyrotrain system had remained closed since the power cut. But on the first day after closure, a large number of workmen had been seen entering Central Station. Everyone assumed they were going to fix the power, yet the station remained closed and the curious little men had not been seen since. No taller than a child, they each had a thick beard and powerful arms and shoulders – these were no ordinary workmen . . .

In a huge antechamber off the ticket hall, a large crowd of these small, menacing figures was being addressed by an even smaller, more menacing, individual . . . it was Maximillion Onyx – and he was a long way from his ornately carved desk at the heart of Onyx Enterprises.

Welcome one and all to the largest gathering of our people ever! Welcome to you my fellow Hypno-Dwarves!

'For centuries it has been hidden, but soon the Lion's Eye will be ours once again! And why now? I hear you ask. Quite simply, I had a brainwave. Rather than search for the *stone* all we had to do was search for the *Stone Dragons* that keep it.'

'Using the financial muscle of Onyx Enterprises I hired the best dragon detectors known to the Mad Monster kingdom – Three-Headed Sniffer Hounds searched far and wide, and they had almost given up when they picked up the scent, right here, right underneath Everyday.'

'I captured the dragons and locked them in a cage. The trouble is they won't tell us the exact location of the stone, but we know it must be near!'

'We needed an excuse to dig, deep, deep under Everyday. A brand new Underground system was the perfect cover, and our state-of-the-art Gyrotrains can go much deeper than any conventional Underground train . . .'

'I would have liked us to work secretly at night when the Gyrotrain system was closed, but as those pesky kids started meddling with the secret door on the opening day I realised we had to move straight to plan B.'

'The "power cut" has kept interfering humans away. And the Hypno-Clocks have worked perfectly. Now no one can stop us from finding our precious stone – NO ONE!!!!'

11

'We need to set our alarm clocks to go off at midnight,' said Zac as he crawled into his sleeping bag. 'I haven't got the energy to fetch mine.'

Odd Dan produced a small, dinosaur-like creature.

'This is a Clockosaurus,' said Odd Dan, winding it up. 'They're excellent time-keepers! But best of all, when they're not screeching, they're fast asleep.'

'Didn't you get a free alarm clock?' asked Zac. 'Everyone in town got one.'

'No one ever delivers anything here since I had a rare Razor-Beaked Snapping Hamster mailed to me,' said Odd Dan as he turned off the light. 'It bit the delivery man's hand so hard that his fingers swelled up like a bunch of bananas.'

Although Zac and Dr Brains weren't quite convinced by the Clockosaurus, they quickly fell asleep. Sure enough, on the stroke of midnight, the prehistoric lizard let off a shriek so loud that Odd Dan's baking tins fell off their shelves with a brain-jangling clatter!

'That's weird,' said Zac. 'We've only slept for four hours but it's still the best sleep I've had in weeks.'

'I don't feel tired at all,' said Dr Brains.

'Let's investigate,' said Zac as they made for the Agency exit.

At first everything seemed normal on the street outside the Agency – the odd alley cat was slinking around, the street lights hummed quietly. But when they turned the corner the sight that greeted them froze them to the core . . .

'The beds . . . they're, they're . . . ALIVE!' gasped Zac. 'What kind of Mad Monster witchcraft is this?'

'The beds have been possessed,' said Odd Dan. 'But who by?'

'And why? Quick, let's follow them!' said Zac.

12

The beds were forming a giant column – they seemed to know exactly where they were going.

'Why aren't people waking up?' asked Zac. 'You'd have thought your bed coming to life and walking out of the house would disturb your sleep a little.'

'Everyone seems to be in an *extremely* deep sleep,' said Odd Dan.

'I would say it's more than that,' said Dr Brains. 'I would go so far as to say they are in some sort of trance . . .'

Zac, Dr Brains and Odd Dan kept a safe distance and it soon became clear that the beds were heading to . . .

The Everyday Gyrotrain station! Outside it was heavily guarded by the short, angry, bearded men.

'Hypno-Dwarves!' said Odd Dan, peering into the darkness at the shadowy figures. 'I should have known!'

'Hypno-Dwarves?!?' asked Zac.

'Gold-digging Dwarves with the power to hypnotise almost anyone – and any*thing*,' said Odd Dan ominously. 'We need to get a closer look at what they are doing.'

'They'll never let us in,' said Zac.

'Unless of course they think we're asleep too,' said Dr Brains. 'Jump on the nearest bed and pretend to sleep!'

'What about this one?' said Odd Dan, who had spotted a large, comfortable-looking bed covered in teddy bears.

'Let's do it!' said Zac.

The Mad Monster Agency team were squashed together in one of the living beds as it marched towards the entrance to the Gyrotrain Station.

'What's that unpleasant rumbling sound?' asked Dr Brains, clinging on.

Zac lifted up a large pink teddy to reveal the bed's snoring owner – Boyston Fitch!

'Nice teddy, tough guy!' chuckled Zac.

'He's dribbling all over me!' complained Odd Dan, mopping his arm. 'The sooner we get inside the better.'

'Under the covers – now!' whispered Zac. 'We're approaching the entrance.'

'The things we do in the line of duty,' winced Dr Brains as the three of them were forced to snuggle up to the snoring, dribbling Boyston.

The guards halted Boyston's bedstead, their suspicions aroused by the number of people crammed on to the teddy-laden bed. But Odd Dan, Zac and Dr Brains gave a good impression of being fast asleep: keeping their eyes tightly shut, despite repeated prodding from a particularly nasty-looking Hypno-Dwarf.

It was a close shave, but it worked – they were in and now maybe they had a chance to get to the bottom of Everyday's sleeping sickness . . .

As each bed slowed to a halt the dozing occupant slowly got up and was handed a pickaxe and shovel . . .

They were then led on to a waiting Gyrotrain which hurtled them deep underground.

Finally stopping in a vast cavern . . .

Everyone was put to work – some digging at the walls, others carrying away the rubble.

All of Everyday seemed to be here.

Working under the watchful eyes of heavily armed Hypno-Dwarves.

'No wonder everyone is exhausted,' said Zac pretending to hack away at the wall, 'when they are spending each night digging. The Hypno-Dwarves must be trying to find the secret location of the Lion's Eye!'

'We've got to stop them before it's too late,' said Odd Dan, pushing a large truck-full of rubble.

'Just as I thought,' said Dr Brains, examining a handful of debris. 'This soil is far too porous for a safe Underground system – the whole place could cave in at any moment!'

13

At the end of their exhausting shift, Zac, Dr Brains and Odd Dan made the uncomfortable trip back home on Boyston's bed.

'I never thought I'd spend time snuggled up to Boyston Fitch,' said Zac as he hid under one of Boyston's huge, cutesy teddies.

'All in the line of duty,' choked Dr Brains, who had Pooky-Wooky's bottom wedged against his face.

When they finally made it back to the Agency, Odd Dan located the necessary Fact File . . .

MAD MONSTER AGENCY FACT FILE:

FULL NAME: Hypno-Dwarves.

TYPE: Hypnotising Dwarves, distant cousins to Mesmerising Munchkins and Brain-Boggling Leprechauns.

AGE: Can live to be over 100 years old. Legend has it that particular Hypno-Dwarves may be IMMORTAL with some iron-smelting Dwarves working FOR EVER in the deepest of all dwarven caverns.

SPECIALITY: Can hypnotise virtually any object and make it do what they want.

FACT: Although once fearsome, these peaceful Mad Monsters have long since given up their violent ways, preferring to quietly mine for gold, out of the way of humans, deep underground.

'They certainly didn't look very peaceful to me!' said Zac.

Before they could consider what might have happened to the Hypno-Dwarves, Dr Brains noticed the time.

'We're going to be late for school!'

'We'll be back later,' said Zac, as he and Dr Brains made their way back upstairs. 'We have to get to the bottom of this!'

After a breakfast of burnt toast and soggy cereal (Josh's parents kept falling asleep), Josh and Spencer made their way to school. Everyday was like a ghost town.

'People are too tired to do anything,' said Josh, as they passed closed shops, empty buses and deserted offices.

'And if you think this is bad, imagine what will happen if the Hypno-Dwarves get their hands on the Lion's Eye,' said Spencer, as they arrived at the school gates.

EVERYDAY SCHOOL

Hardly anyone had turned up for school, but somehow Boyston had pulled himself out of his bed.

'Hey losers, you feeling tired?' asked Boyston. 'There must be Mad Monsters behind this, and me and the crew are going to sort them out tonight!'

'I suppose you'll be taking Pooky-Wooky with you?' chuckled Josh. 'He'll scare the Mad Monsters . . .'

Boyston's crew couldn't help chuckling.

'What are you talking about?' barked Boyston turning scarlet as he lunged for Josh and Spencer, but fortunately he was interrupted by the school bell.

At assembly the Headmistress, who looked even more exhausted than before, stood up to address the pupils.

'There are no announcements today,' she yawned. 'Instead we will all have a sleep . . . I'll just set my alarm clock for half an hour . . .'

'Wait a moment,' whispered Josh, as everyone snoozed, 'the alarm clock, I think I get it . . .'

'Get what?' said Spencer.

'We've all been given one – right?' said Josh. 'A free gift, out of the blue . . .'

'Yes, but I still don't get it,' said Spencer.

'Ever since the people of Everyday have had their new alarm clocks we've all been tired! There's something we need to do when we get back from school . . .'

14

When the sleepy school day came to an end, Josh and Spencer went back to Josh's house as fast as they could. They stepped over Josh's parents, who were sleeping in the hall, and went straight up to Josh's bedroom.

'I should never have trusted this thing,' said Josh, grabbing his alarm clock.

With it tucked firmly under his arm Josh flew down the chute and into the Agency, swiftly followed by Spencer . . .

'So are we heading over to the Gyrotrain station to sort out those Hypno-Dwarves?' said Odd Dan, who as usual was wide awake and fully energised.

'Not quite yet,' said Zac. 'We need to work on a plan of attack. But first of all let's take a closer look at this.'

'A clock?' said a bemused Odd Dan.

'Be careful,' said Zac, placing the alarm clock on a work bench. 'I don't trust that thing . . .'

Dr Brains, using his curse-proof screwdriver, cautiously removed the back – and at once noticed a tiny insignia.

'What does it say?' asked Zac. Dr Brains squinted through a magnifying glass.

'It seems to be a company name . . . yes, I can just make it out: the Onyx Corporation!'

'The Onyx Corporation, Maximillion Onyx, Hypno-Dwarves – somehow it must all tie up,' said Zac. 'But how? Odd Dan, do you have any more information on Onyx?'

'The Onyx Corporation is involved in mining, oil drilling and underground construction worldwide,' said Odd Dan.

'Sounds like Maximillion Onyx likes his business to be conducted in a subterranean fashion,' said Dr Brains.

'Yes, everything he does seems to involve some form of digging,' said Odd Dan.

'So do we know who he really is?' asked Zac.

'I feel like I've heard the name Maximillion Onyx somewhere else,' mused Dr Brains. 'Recently.'

'Maximillion Onyx . . . Max Onyx – hang on,' said Zac, his eyes lighting up. 'What was the name of the ancient king who once terrorised the world with the Lion's Eye?'

'The king in Snardvark's story? Wasn't it King Noymaxx III?' said Dr Brains.

'This is no made-up fairytale king, this is real – "Noymaxx" is an anagram of Max Onyx!' said Zac. 'Odd Dan, Fact Files please – do we have a King Noymaxx III?'

After much searching of the cabinets, Odd Dan returned with a Fact File.

'I think we've just made a huge breakthrough,' he said handing over the file.

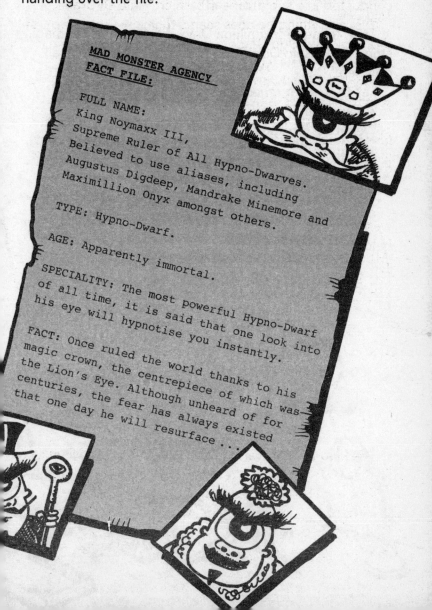

MAD MONSTER AGENCY
FACT FILE:

FULL NAME:
King Noymaxx III,
Supreme Ruler of All Hypno-Dwarves.
Believed to use aliases, including
Augustus Digdeep, Mandrake Minemore and
Maximillion Onyx amongst others.

TYPE: Hypno-Dwarf.

AGE: Apparently immortal.

SPECIALITY: The most powerful Hypno-Dwarf
of all time, it is said that one look into
his eye will hypnotise you instantly.

FACT: Once ruled the world thanks to his
magic crown, the centrepiece of which was
the Lion's Eye. Although unheard of for
centuries, the fear has always existed
that one day he will resurface ...

15

'So that explains why the Hypno-Dwarves have returned!' said Zac.

'Their leader, Maximillion Onyx, finally wants his magic stone back,' said Odd Dan. 'And if he finds it we're all doomed!'

'Let's see what other secrets the clock has to yield,' said Zac urgently.

'Well it's a typical alarm clock movement,' said Dr Brains. 'Beautifully made, but nothing unusual here . . . except –'

'Except?' said Zac eagerly.

'There is a small speaker device in here. The workmanship really is remarkable,' said Dr Brains, as he held up the tiny speaker.

'Why would you put a speaker in an alarm clock?' said Zac. 'I've only ever heard it ring.'

'It seems to have a timing dial of its own,' said Dr Brains. 'It's set to go off at midnight . . . Unless I just press the overide button right here . . .'

A quiet but insistent voice could be heard: *'You are feeling very tired . . . you cannot move . . . you cannot open your eyes . . .'*

'It's starting to hypnotise us,' said Zac, as his eyes glazed over. 'We've . . . got . . . to . . . stop . . . it . . .'

'I'm . . . feeling . . . very . . . tired . . .' said Dr Brains, as he slumped across the work bench. 'I . . . am . . . falling . . .'

'Hey! My furniture is starting to come to life!' said Odd Dan, wrestling with his bed. 'Oh no you don't!'

Odd Dan pinned down the bed and managed to aim an Eccles cake at the alarm, smashing it to pieces. The voice stopped and Zac and Dr Brains started to come out of their daze.

'That was close,' said Dr Brains, rubbing his eyes.

'Good thing I was ready with some Kung Food,' said Odd Dan. Kung Food is an ancient martial art that uses buns, cakes, cookies and all manner of home-baked goods as weapons.

'We strike tonight!' said Zac. 'It's time to put the Hypno-Dwarves and the Onyx Corporation to bed – FOR EVER! We just need to figure out how . . .'

16

'I've had a great idea for a gadget,' said Dr Brains holding up the tiny speaker. 'A gadget that the Hypno-Dwarves will be powerless against!'

'Great, Brains, but hold that idea. There's something else we need if we're going to take them on underground,' said Zac.

'Yikes,' whimpered Odd Dan. 'All those dark tunnels, danger around every corner.'

'Exactly,' said Zac. 'Which is why we're going to need a map and I know exactly where we can get one. Odd Dan, you come with me. Dr Brains, get to work – we need your gadget to be ready by the time we get back.'

With Dr Brains frantically assembling a Hypno-Dwarf-busting gadget, Odd Dan and Zac were in the Mad Monstermobile speeding across town.

'Boyston Fitch's house!' gasped Odd Dan, when Zac told him where they were going. 'But why?'

'The Gyrotrain station is heavily guarded,' said Zac. 'If we're going to infiltrate it, we need an edge.'

'But Boyston is rubbish at Mad Monster hunting,' said Odd Dan, as they pulled up next to Boyston's house. 'How can he possibly help us?'

'He can't, but his father can,' said Zac. 'Boyston said that Mr Fitch was involved in the construction of the Gyrotrain system. He's got plans and maps . . . and with any luck the whole Fitch family should be fast asleep!'

'What now?' asked Odd Dan. 'You can't just ring the doorbell.'

'No, but it looks like there's an open window,' said Zac squinting through the windscreen. 'The Mad Monstermobile winch should do the trick.'

As Zac hoped, everyone in the Fitch household was snoring. Using the Mad Monstermobile's winch, Odd Dan lowered Zac through the open window.

Once inside, Zac began gingerly searching for the maps.
Why do floorboards have to be so creaky? he thought,
as every step seemed to make a deafening groan.
Fortunately the noise of the floorboards was drowned
out by a loud, rasping sound. Boyston. Pausing just long
enough to sneak a peek at the snoring bully and his
teddies, Zac carried on his search.

He was about to give up when he noticed a sliding door.

'What's in here?' he wondered, as he slid the door
back. The room was full of maps and plans. He saw a
computer and a desk with piles of books.

Bingo! Mr Fitch's study! thought Zac. And there, tucked
under some books, were the maps!

Using his Mad Monster spy camera Zac quickly took
some pictures.

Now all he had to do was get out. With the family still
snoring, Zac let himself out through the front door as
quietly as he could.

17

'This is great,' said Odd Dan as they zoomed back to the Agency. 'I've never seen so little traffic. Not even a hint of the usual rush hour.'

'That's because everyone is in their beds exhausted,' said Zac as he scanned the map. He couldn't believe what he was seeing. 'You'd have thought that the Mayor's office would have asked questions about all these extra tunnels and rooms when they were constructing the Gyrotrain.'

'No one who asks Maximillion Onyx any difficult questions lasts very long,' said Odd Dan.

'There has got to be another way in . . .' said Zac grimly.

Back at the Agency Dr Brains was putting some finishing touches to his gadget. He proudly pressed a button and a screen glided up at the front of the workshop to reveal a large metallic object.

'Behold the Hypno-Mega-Blaster!' said Brains.

'It looks like a giant hearing-aid,' said Odd Dan as they walked around the device.

'Hearing will certainly be involved,' said Dr Brains proudly. 'But it will be the Hypno-Dwarves doing it. You see, I've wired up the speaker from the alarm clock and it will blast out their hypnotic message at over 1000 decibels. While you were gone, I synthesised the voice from the alarm clock – anyone who hears it will go into a deep trance and be rooted to the spot!'

'Great!' said Zac. 'But what about us? Won't we be hypnotised too?'

'Not with these,' said Dr Brains, revealing another gadget. 'I call them Hypno-Muffs. I've set them to block out the Blaster.'

Zac and the team assembled at the Agency table.

'I have a plan,' said Zac. 'Gentlemen, look at the screen.'

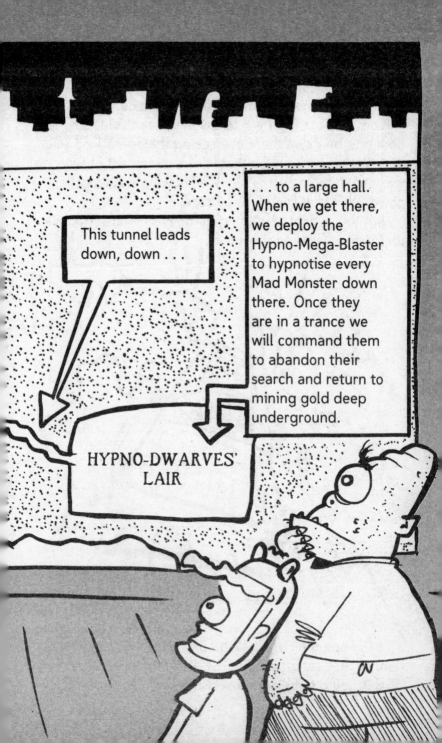

'That should put the Hypno-Dwarves out of action,' said Dr Brains. 'But what about their leader, what about Maximillion Onyx? We don't know where he is . . .'

'From his Fact File I would say he's a control freak. He's bound to be down there overseeing the operation,' said Zac. 'We've got to hope that with the element of surprise we catch him unawares too. We know he's the most powerful Hypno-Dwarf, so be careful.'

With the gadget loaded on to the Mad Monstermobile the Agency were on the move.

'Let's hope the Hypno-Mega-Blaster works,' said Odd Dan, as they set off for Snardvark Threebellies' cave. 'This is going to be our most risky Mad Monster Mission yet.'

18

Deep underground the Hypno-Dwarves were preparing
for the night ahead – with an address from their leader
Maximillion Onyx.

'We are getting close my friends, very close,' said the
evil tycoon. 'I can feel it, I can smell it, I can SENSE IT!
The Lion's Eye is only a shovel away.'

The Hypno-Dwarves cheered.

'But we must redouble our efforts,' he continued. 'The tunnels cannot support the digging for much longer, and if they are to collapse then our precious jewel will be lost for ever! Imagine, no lovely shiny, glittery stone. No way to take over the world . . . So tonight I want the people of Everyday to work EXTRA hard!'

19

When they got to Snardvark's cave, they had to knock and knock before she finally arrived at the door.

'It's tho sthtrange,' said Snardvark as she ushered them in. 'No matter how long I sthleep I sthtill wake up tired.'

'This might put a stop to your all-day snoozing,' said Zac, spotting an Onyx Corporation alarm clock by Snardvark's bedside. He picked it up and then smashed it on the floor.

'But, but . . . I loved that clock,' said Snardvark. 'It was beautiful.'

Zac explained what was going on – and as soon as she understood Snardvark was only too happy to help.

'Well of courth I am a bit ruthsty,' said the dragon. 'It'th been a long time sinth I used my breath for exthcavation.'

The team were back in the Mad Monstermobile and, using the map, they soon located the air vent. As Zac had predicted it was firmly shut – it was over to Snardvark. Breathing in deeply the dragon took aim and with a ground-shuddering burst of flame blew the air vent grille clean off.

'I think that will do it,' said Snardvark, whose snout was still smoking. 'And I've got the perfect rope to get us down there . . .'

20

With the way in blasted open, it was time for the most dangerous part of the mission yet. Zac and the team began lowering themselves down into the ticket hall.

'Are you sure this cord is strong enough?' wailed Odd Dan.

'It's thuper-thrength Dwarf-beard rope,' said Snardvark reassuringly, as they made their way into the dimly lit, silent hall.

'We've got to move quickly,' whispered Zac, locating the small, intricately carved door that they'd first noticed on the day of the Grand Opening. The hornet's nest of Hypno-Dwarves was only a tunnel away.

Zac went first. He gently pushed the door and it creaked open . . . revealing a narrow tunnel.

'Just big enough for Hypno-Dwarves so I guess we'll be crawling,' said Zac. 'Be ready – when we get there, there will be some pretty angry Mad Monsters waiting for us!'

As they squeezed their way along the tunnel, it felt very unstable. The wooden struts holding up the roof groaned under the weight of the ground above them.

'I was right,' said Dr Brains. 'This place can't take a lot more digging.'

'Luckily I brought the Therpent's Thapphire with me. It's magic allows me to thlither through the thmallest plathes,' said Snardvark proudly.

'Keep your voices down,' hissed Zac. 'The element of surprise is essential to our plan.'

The tunnel wound its way deeper and deeper underground until gradually they could make out the sound of machinery . . . they turned a corner and there was a bright light. Crawling as quietly as they could, they reached the end of the tunnel. They were now at the top of a staircase leading to a vast hall . . .

They had found the Dwarves' inner sanctum! Dozens of Hypno-Dwarves were methodically sifting through piles of rubble – searching for their precious stone. Using the power of hypnosis, rocks were being lifted and dumped without a hand so much as touching them . . .

Although fascinated by the scene unfolding beneath him, the team knew they didn't have much time.

'Dr Brains, prime the Hypno-Mega-Blaster,' whispered Zac. 'Odd Dan and Snardvark, you stand guard – don't let the Hypno-Dwarves anywhere near it.'

'Don't forget your Hypno-Muffs,' said Dr Brains, handing every member of the team a pair.

'I've got to grab their attention and hope that they follow me here,' said Zac, slipping on his Hypno-Muffs. With that he snatched a flaming torch and began the descent to the Dwarves' hall.

21

As soon as Zac got to the foot of the stairs, all eyes were on the intruder.

At first there was confusion, then rocks started raining down on him – he'd got their attention all right! Dodging the rocks and boulders that were flying his way, Zac jumped up and down and waved his hands.

'The game's up!' cried Zac. 'Why don't you just give up – you'll never find your gemstone!'

As he had hoped, the Hypno-Dwarves, furious at this invasion, were soon in hot pursuit . . .

Zac started climbing back up the stairs – with the Hypno-Dwarves getting ever closer . . . He felt them grabbing his legs from behind him but he was able to kick himself free. Finally he reached the top – and Dr Brains' gadget. It was time to see if it worked!

'The Hypno-Mega-Blaster!' he shouted. 'NOW!!!'

Dr Brains was about to switch the machine on when he began to feel sleepy . . . the Hypno-Dwarves were trying to hypnotise them!

'There are too many of them . . .' said Dr Brains sleepily. 'The Hypno-Muffs can't cope . . .'

'*You are feeling very sleepy . . .*' the Hypno-Dwarves said in their deep, quietly comforting voices. '*You are drifting . . . drifting away . . .*'

'Must . . . not . . . fall . . . asleep,' said Zac desperately, as he fought against the overwhelming longing to slip into a deep sleep.

They were all just about to start snoring when a small precious stone crashed down on the head of the lead Hypno-Dwarf.

'Take that!' bellowed a voice from behind them – it was Snardvark! 'Good thing I brought the Fabnabulous Emerald of Effulgia with me!'

'Push the dial on the Hypno-Mega-Blaster to maximum!' shouted Zac urgently.

Blinking and breathing in deeply, Dr Brains switched the machine on . . .

As the voice echoed loudly through the hall, at first the Hypno-Dwarves seemed confused . . . but just as Zac and the team had hoped, the Hypno-Mega-Blaster was working, and one by one Hypno-Dwarves' eyes glazed

over and they stood frozen to the spot – hypnotised!
The cavern was now quiet and still – all the Hypno-
Dwarves simply stood where they were, staring into
space.

'That was close,' said Odd Dan. 'Good thing Snardvark had that emerald to hand.'

'And my gadget worked!' said Dr Brains proudly as he switched off the Hypno-Mega-Blaster. But before the Agency could order the Hypno-Dwarves to resume their peaceful lives underground they heard a deafening crash.

'What was that?' said Odd Dan nervously.

'The door at the back of the hall – someone has escaped through it,' said Dr Brains. One Hypno-Dwarf was going to be harder to subdue.

'Maximillion Onyx!' said Zac. 'This mission is not over yet . . .'

22

'So Maximillion Onyx is immune to the Hypno-Mega-Blaster,' said Dr Brains. 'I underestimated his powers. We'll need to put the Hypno-Muffs on a higher setting.'

'I don't like the sound of this,' said Odd Dan. 'I've seen enough Mad Monsters for one night.'

'There was no doorway shown on the map,' said Zac. 'Beyond that door must be Maximillion Onyx's top-secret hideout. And we're going to have to flush him out.'

'We don't have long,' said Dr Brains, as a few pieces of earth rained down from the ceiling. 'The place could cave in at any moment!'

'Well it's not the most welcoming entrance I've ever seen,' said Odd Dan, as he heaved and heaved. The door finally creaked open . . . to reveal yet another tunnel. They were about to go through the door when a voice boomed from the other side of the hall.

'Snardvark, is that you? Please help us!'

'What was that?' asked Zac.

The Hypno-Dwarves remained motionless.

'It's coming from over there,' said Dr Brains, pointing to the edge of a metal cage almost buried under the rubble.

'I think I know what's under there,' said Snardvark. 'I'll investigate and catch up with you.'

Zac, Dr Brains and Odd Dan were now crawling and winding their way ever deeper underground. All was horribly quiet, although every now and then the ground shuddered and timber props creaked and groaned. Some tunnels were very steep and dark, lit only by the glimmer of Dwarf torches.

'Trolls aren't built for creeping through tunnels,' muttered Odd Dan. 'Nasty narrow places, tunnels.'

Eventually they got to the end of one particularly narrow tunnel, and this one opened out into another vast hall . . .

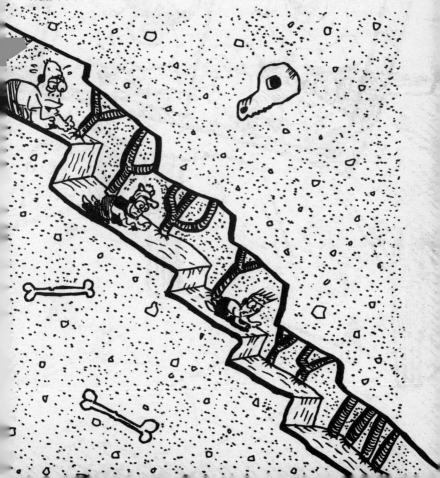

'So this is his lair,' said Zac. 'He's now trying to hypnotise the whole world!'

Sure enough, Onyx was booming out his message: 'SLEEEEEP! SLEEEEEP! YOU ARE FEELING *VERY* DROWSY! YOUR BODY IS HEAVYYYYYYYYYY!'

'How are we going to take him off air?' asked Dr Brains. 'There are Hypno-Dwarf guards everywhere. And we have no Hypno-Mega-Blaster.'

'My Kung Food will never work on all of them,' said Odd Dan.

'We've got to stop him transmitting,' said Zac. 'We need to pull the plug on Maximillion Onyx once and for all . . .'

'A diversion!' said Zac. 'Something that will grab the guards' attention. Something that will give us the chance to get past them.'

'Maybe Scarab could help?' suggested Dr Brains, holding up a jar. 'He comes with me everywhere. All Scarab and his fellow Wereroaches want is to be left in peace underground – I'm sure he'd love to put an end to the Hypno-Dwarves and their constant digging!'

'But he's tiny!' said Zac. 'He won't be able to do it on his own.'

'Remember the Fact File,' Dr Brains beamed. 'Wereroaches have huge strength in numbers . . .'

23

'I'll have to set the Mad Monster Trans-Species-Inter-Communicator to hyper-drive,' said Dr Brains, adjusting the knob on his brain helmet. 'It's one thing doing tricks at Show and Tell – but this is dangerous work.'

'Keep that thing away from me!' wheedled Odd Dan, who was cowering behind a boulder.

With Scarab fully briefed he let out a high-pitched whistle. At first nothing happened, then the ground began to shake . . . Soon dozens of Wereroaches began to emerge from every corner of the cave. It was time to take on the Hypno-Dwarves and drive out Maximillion Onyx!

The first task was to get through the front line of the Dwarf defences, and the mini Mad Monsters were soon nipping and biting the Hypno-Dwarf guards, who didn't have the stomach for taking on an angry Wereroach and his friends, and soon scattered . . .

Once through the guards they had to battle their way up a steep flight of stairs, ducking attacks from Dwarf bowmen hidden in caves high up in the walls . . .

And after Odd Dan knocked out two snarling wild boars (the Dwarf King's pets) with a well-aimed banana biscuit (home-made of course!) – they made it to Maximillion Onyx's podium!

And there he was – glaring into a great bank of cameras with his single eye, broadcasting his hypnotic message world-wide!

'Shield your eyes!' cried Zac.

'You cannot stop me!' boomed Onyx. 'Guards, grab them!'

But his guards were cowering – terrified of the vicious Wereroach hordes snarling at them.

'You too will soon be under my spell and the search for the Lion's Eye will be complete!' scoffed Onyx, pulling a cord. 'Open the escape hatch, time to use the Gyrocopter.'

A huge opening appeared high in the hall above them. In the far distance they could see the night sky.

Onyx had stepped on to his Gyrocopter and lifted off – a large speaker booming out his hypno-message . . .

'YOU ARE FEELING SLEEPY! YOU WANT TO DRIFT AWAY! YOU WILL SOON BE UNDER MY CONTROL!'

'He's getting away!' shouted Zac desperately.

24

All seemed lost when suddenly they heard a BOOM and then the flapping of leathery wings – it was Snardvark, swooping down from a large opening in the roof!

'We'll take him down in no time!' said Snardvark.

'We?' said Zac, looking around.

'As I thought, trapped in that cage were thome old friends,' said Snardvark. 'The legendary Thtone Dragons! But they would never tell Onyx where the thtone was . . . Together we blathted our way in here. Dangerous – but we had to do it!'

Behind Snardvark were three huge dragons, flailing their mighty wings.

'Quick – hop onboard.'

With each member of the Mad Monster Agency team on the back of a dragon they were soon in hot pursuit of Maximillion Onyx's Gyrocopter.

'Get those beasts away from me!' squealed Onyx. 'My quest will not be foiled!'

'Snardvark!' shouted Zac above the sound of the dragons' thrashing wings. 'How do we bring down that Dwarf-king?'

'There is only one way,' said Snardvark, as she circled the Onyx Gyrocopter. 'You, Thac, must hypnotise Onyx! Look behind my left ear.'

'What's this?' asked Zac, holding up a heavy stone box. 'It weighs a ton!'

'It is the Lion's Eye,' said Snardvark. 'The Thtone Dragons found it for me. The Hypno-Dwarves were even clother to finding the thtone than they thought.'

'*You* have the Lion's Eye?' said Zac.

'Yeth and this plathe is about to collapth. We've got to sthtop him now!' said Snardvark.

'If you can get close to Onyx, I'll walk along your wing and blast him with the Lion's Eye!' said Zac

With that Snardvark swooped in as close to the Gyrocopter as she dared.

Zac began the perilous walk along Snardvark's wing . . . Once he reached the end he was face to face with Maximillion Onyx.

'You dare approach *me*!' he cackled.

'You don't scare me!' said Zac. 'Is this what you've been looking for?'

As soon as Zac opened the box, there was an incredible flash of amber light.

Zac screwed up his eyes and looked away. But Maximillion Onyx didn't react so quickly . . .

. . . his hideous eye glazed over and he slumped at the controls.

The Gyrocopter started to spin frantically but Odd Dan and Brains commanded the Stone Dragons to bring the 'copter down to the cave floor. In seconds Odd Dan and Brains had tied up Onyx with Dwarf-beard rope. One of the Stone Dragons gave a flick of its great tail to smash the Gyrocopter to smithereens.

The Mad Monster Agency had saved the day!

With Maximillion hypnotised by the Lion's Eye, Zac and his team were able to clear the tunnels and halls as quickly as possible. Zac could finally command the entranced Hypno-Dwarves to return to peacefully mining for gold.

'Great work, Snardvark, we couldn't have done it without you,' said Zac. 'Now take Mr Onyx, or should I say King Noymaxx III to Mad Monster Island Prison!'

'That's very kind,' said Snardvark. 'Now jump on my back – this plathe is going to crumble any second!'

25

'Let's get busy in the kitchen,' said Odd Dan
energetically, when they were back at the Agency. 'Who
fancies a batch of my triple-choc muffins?!'

'I think I'm going to have a sleep,' said Zac, rubbing
his eyes.

'Yes,' yawned Dr Brains. 'For a looooong time.'

Even Odd Dan decided that a siesta would be a good idea – and the team all slept soundly in the knowledge that they had once again saved the world from Mad Monsters.

Still in a spell, Maximillion Onyx finally agreed to end his quest. He was sent to the remotest Mad Monster prison, where he joined the Prison Showbiz Society as their star hypnotist.

The people of Everyday soon recovered their energy – even Mr Derrick. In fact he'd never been busier – collecting everybody's alarm clocks and delivering them straight to the Everyday dump!

TRAMLINE COMING SOON

The Gyrotrain system was condemned as unsafe, and plans were drawn up for an Everyday tramline.

The Lion's Eye was returned to the Stone Dragons, who promised to continue guarding it deep underground for evermore.

And Boyston Fitch? Well, he was still his normal annoying self. He finally stopped sleeping with Pooky-Wooky (although he still keeps his favourite teddy close at hand on his bedside table . . .)

But back at the Agency, the eyes on the ivory skull of Zebadiah Zoltan's favourite walking stick started to glow red . . . Time for another mission for Zac Zoltan's Mad Monster Agency!

Bonus Features

The Mad Monster History of The
World Part 2: The Lion's Eye

Spotlight on Snardvark Threebellies'
Collection of Mad Monster Gemstones

Blueprint of the Mad Monstermobile

A Life in the Day of Balthasar
Boarback, a Typical Hypno-Dwarf

The Lion's Eye

For centuries Mad Monsters waged wars to get their hands on the famed jewel the Lion's Eye and the immense power it brings . . .

At different times it has been in the hands of many Mad Monsters. **The Singing Squids** of the South Pacific, used it to enslave all things sea-bound and force them to listen to their terrible underwater warblings.

The **Goat-Headed Herdsmen** of the Himalayas used its magic to turn their alpine fortresses into a goat's paradise.

Until finally, it came into the hands of a young king with astonishing hypnotic powers, the Hypno-Dwarf **Noymaxx III**.

The Lion's Eye took pride of place amongst the sparkling jewels in his magnificent crown and soon all of humanity was forced to satisfy King Noymaxx's most outlandish whims.

This would have carried on for ever had it not been for one brave, young Hypno-Dwarf. **Tonelius Topaz**. He alone could see how Noymaxx's desire for power was ruining the Hypno-Dwarves (who had always been peace-loving gold miners).

He set out to find the only Mad Monsters resistant to the jewel – the legendary **Stone Dragons**. His mission took him deep, deep underground. He crossed gorges of molten lava and fled swarms of ravenous Wereroaches . . .

Finally he found the Stone Dragons and they agreed to venture out into what they called 'Upstairs Land'. After a fearsome battle with hordes of Noymaxx's hypnotised minions they finally wrested the Lion's Eye from King Noymaxx's crown . . . And determined to keep it safe for evermore . . .

Spotlight on Snardvark Threebellies' Collection of Mad Monster Gemstones

The Emerald Ring of Erimatrea
– this ring enables the wearer to turn any shade of green – very handy for hiding in forests!

The Serpent's Sapphire – allows the owner to slither through the narrowest hole and disappear into the most inaccessible places.

The Amethyst Crown
– weighs over 7 tonnes, so it is unwise to try it on (unless you happen to be a giant).

The Bloodstone Belt Buckle of Byzantium – once adorned a queen's coronation robes but was stolen by a well-trained Burglar Baboon and has disappeared into legend.

The Monarch Moonstone – the largest moonstone ever discovered. It sits in the belly button of Zupedax Graawn, the mightiest of the Stone Dragons.

And these are just a few of the gemstones from my fabnabulous collection!

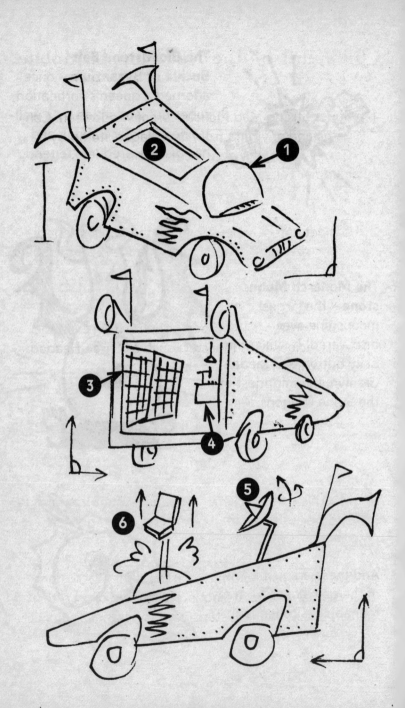

Blueprint of the Mad Monstermobile

1   Super Strong Mad Monster-proof windscreen. Can withstand anything from an enraged stomp by a Gargle Giant to a peck from the beak of a Sledge-hammer Falcon.

2   Gadget-hatch – opens to allow the deployment of super-sized anti-Mad-Monster Gadgets (with labelled examples).

3   Mad Monster holding pen – can restrain even the most vicious Mad Monsters such as Three-Headed Stoats or Berserk Beard Badgers.

4   Mini-workshop – fully kitted-out to allow Dr Brains to make vital final adjustments to gadgets.

5   Mad Monster tracker – this radar system can pick up and track certain Mad Monsters.

6   Ejector seats – for immediate cockpit evacuation: essential when battling incredibly big or incredibly small Mad Monsters (e.g. Skyscraper Toads or Weenybeetles).

A Life in the Day of Balthasar Boarback, a Typical Hypno-Dwarf

It's great being able to hypnotise objects. It means when I wake up I can make a cup of coffee, feed the cat and shower without even leaving my bed!

At work I like to have a break mid-morning and go to the gym. I find it's useful to give the eyeball a good workout, and I mostly lift weights.

When I go out, I like to look my best – combing my thick beard and moustache is easy and I can watch TV and read the paper at the same time.

My hobby is darts – I can play sitting down while still holding a foaming flagon of mead.

At the end of the day I like to cook – tossing pancakes and spinning pizzas couldn't be easier!